Rose Blanche Woodyear, Howard Chandler Christy

In Camphor

Rose Blanche Woodyear, Howard Chandler Christy

In Camphor

ISBN/EAN: 9783337422783

Printed in Europe, USA, Canada, Australia, Japan

Cover: Foto ©Andreas Hilbeck / pixelio.de

More available books at **www.hansebooks.com**

IN CAMPHOR

PUBLISHED BY G. P. PUT-
NAM'S SONS, MDCCCXCV
NEW YORK

The Knickerbocker Press, New York

They were woven of sorrow,
  Thread by thread,
From a heart wounded and bleeding
  For its dead.

The strong arm leaned on,
  Tender and brave ;
The precious child-daughter ;
  Both in the grave.

CONTENTS.

7

IN CAMPHOR

IN CAMPHOR.

THEY are all put away in camphor now,
    The soft warm wraps and the furs ;
She wore them in hours of happiest play,
    These garments, so dear, that were hers.

I 've folded them down with a mother's tears,
    The little frocks spotless and white ;
And locked them up in her own little trunk,
    With her dolls—shut out from my sight.

With sighs such only as mothers can breathe,
    Which none but the Wound-binder heard,
I 've closed the door to her dear little room,
    Empty cage that has lost its bird.

11

I sit and wonder how mothers can live
　　Through death's awful shock—the first blow,
And how in calm faith they can give God back
　　The child He in love did bestow.

And then I wonder what power can keep
　　The moth-eating grief from my heart;
Not the sorrowful past to put to sleep,
　　But healing and health to impart.

If the gum that comes from a wounded tree
　　Can drive away moth from the chest,
Will not the balm that from Calvary flowed
　　Drive sorrow and care from my breast?

And so I 've been packing these clothes away
   With the gum of the fragrant tree,
And will let Him fill my poor careworn heart,
   With His peace,—like perfume to me.

And thus till I reach the home-garden fair
   Where the sweet camphor blossom grows,
The balm that comes from that same Camphor Tree
   Shall be solace for all my woes.

THE KEY TO THE CAMPHOR CHEST.

FAINT ring at the door-bell.
  " A child," my sad heart said.
" The hand is small and
      trembling,
  Or weak for want of bread."

And when the bell was answered,
  A child scarce ten years old—
Whose clothes were thin and
      threadbare—
  Stood shivering in the cold.

14

Two little shoes with toes out,
　　Two little hands both red,
Oh, dear sad eyes, how wistful,
　　Longing, yet filled with dread.

"If you 've some clothes for children,"—
　　She seemed quite dumb from fear—
"You see I have n't any "—
　　And waiting, dropped a tear.

This lowly child I looked at ;
　　"The camphor chest "—I said,
"Its soft warm furs and clothing
　　Not needed by my dead."

I took her hand—'t was trembling,
    And led her to the chest ;
Must I unlock my heart's grief
    To help this child—God's guest ?

I took a soft warm bonnet,
    With fresh bow knots of lace,
And tying on I whispered,
    "Let mother keep that face!"

Her cold thin hands transparent
    These gloves seemed just to fit ;
Her sweet eyes lost their sadness,
    And smiles began to flit.

Shoes hardly worn and stockings,
  Soft flannels, frocks and furs,—
" You, little girl, are welcome ;
  All of them once were hers."

The chest will soon be empty,
  For love has found the key ;
I hear Him gently whisper,.
  "Ye did it unto Me."

A LITTLE HAND.

ARE you kind and quick at discerning things?
　　Can you see on the window pane
The print of a dear little dimpled hand,
　　Between the dried drops of rain?

The storm has splashed on the outer side,
　　The glass has been polished within;
Yet thus always the print of that dear little hand,
　　Be there sunlight or shadow dim.

18

Its tapers point up to the Hand it caught,
    Somewhere—up there in the day—
And I know that His clasp is tighter far
    Than mine could be, here on the way.

So this dear little hand that points the way,
    Holds the helm in my boat of time,
And when sailing is done and life's sea crossed,
    That same little hand will clasp mine.

HEARTSEASE.

IMPETUOUS words are on my lips;
  My heart is always sad—
Will the scars of sorrow ever heal,
  And in healing make me glad?

My heart's world now is only dust;
  My roses are but ashes;
Will the coming years be years of woe,
  And tears still on my lashes?

The voice in the wind—its charm has gone;
　The tone of the rustling leaf;
The shaded walks where the paths entwined,
　Disenchanted of all—but grief.

If a veil has fallen o'er mine eyes
　Shutting out the light of the sun,
And I can follow Him in the dark,
　Has a new walk not begun?

Is not the infinite wisdom of God
　Taking the dross from the gold,
Showing His wondrous love for me
　While leading me on to His fold?

HEARTSEASE.

If hope has vanished like a mist,
  And the skies are overcast,
Can I not live with patience then,
  Till I reach my home at last?

If roses were always roses here,
  And hearts were never sad,
In the whirl and rush of thoughtless joy
  Would not the world go mad?

Then let us work and wait and trust,
  With childlike love and fear;
Though dust and ashes at His feet,
  Our hearts He yet will cheer.

For ashes He 'll give beauty then,
  For weakness He 'll give strength,
Our very tears He 'll change to pearls,
  And Heartsease come at length.

KEEP THEM HAPPY.

H, where shall I go with my sorrow,
    In secret to weep out my woe?
Youth must not e'en guess at my sighing,
    Or my heart's joyless depths ever know.

Not heartless because they are happy,
    They 're just unacquainted with grief,
Who then would hush their light laughter,
    When unshadowed days are so brief?

25

There 's a charm in sweet womanhood's morning,
 In the joyous key of her song,
That will echo through life till the evening,
 Though her days be sad and long.

So regal is true-hearted manhood,
 As he girds on his sword for the fight,
So dauntless in lofty courage,
 There 's naught can withstand his might.

She 's like a rosebud of summer,
 And he like a twig of the oak,
For me the stem had borne blossom and fruit,
 Ere it drooped with its burden and broke.

Their tears will come sooner or later,
Just when none ever can know,
And we, too, shall sigh our last sorrow,
And in heaven forget our past woe.

Then pave not their path with pebbles,
But line their life-walk with flowers,
Blossoms, and buds, and rose-leaves,
Freshened by sweet-scented showers.

Blight not a hope they are building,
 Hush not a note that they sing,
We once had our own " air castles,"
 And all the bright promise of Spring.

MY BELOVED.

I SAW and kissed his kind sweet face,
　　And touched his silvered hair,
Our lovely child stood at his side,
　　Gentle, tender, fair.

I saw his dear lips move in smiles,
　　Love light his brilliant eye,
The same rich voice I heard again,
　　Just as in days gone by.

29

I saw her white arms clasp him round
  In tender love and care,
Her shining hair fell like a veil,
  And hid her face so fair.

And then a change, and all was strange,
  And I deep pain could feel,
For I awoke, 't was only sleep,
  The pain and change were real.

PRAYER.

THE prayer that went unanswered
  Did not prove the wish unheard,
It only told some better plan,
  Or else of hope deferred.

Then waiting need never discourage,
  Nor withholding take away faith,
So still thy heart's complaining,
  And wait, the Master saith.

THEN AND NOW.

THEN I *hoped* " whatever is is right,"
  And I had for my reason why
Each wish granted, happiness possessed,
  And I thought, Who 's happier than I ?

But now I *know* " whatever is is right,"
  And I have for my reason why,
Faith and hope, more than I can express,
  Oh ! who can be happier than I ?

THE TWO BIRTHDAYS.

IN counting her heavenly birthdays,
One, two years old to-day;
Though were she here beside me,
We 'd count thirteen this May.

In heaven she 's been but a morning,
On earth she did not reach noon;
To my white rose, my tender bud,
Both birthdays came so soon.

33

Before we had thought of danger,
  Dark shades shot 'cross the light ;
A hush fell on her laughter,
  And turned our day to night.

'T was the very first hour of Good Friday,
  Her soul passed into the light,
And we laid her in silent Greenmount
  Between Easter-noon and night.

And now on these two birthdays,
  Of heaven and of earth,
We wreathe together May flowers,
  And lilies of Easter birth.

And wend our way with arms full—
　　Her dear ones gathering round—
With the freshest, sweetest flowers
　　To lay on that little mound.

In His garden gathering lilies,
　　Reaping what she has sown,
The broken buds of earth exchanged
　　For heaven's fair flowers full blown.

MEMORIES.

WREATHE me a garland of roses rare,
Wreathe for the grave of my darling there,
Lace them together the bud and the leaf,
Fair as the day, yet emblems of grief.

Listening, I hear her voice in the air ;
Waiting oft fancy her step on the stair ;
Memory brings her form to my side,
As though it was only this morn she died.

36

"I hear her step on the stair."

Oft I can feel her kiss on my cheek,
　Hear her light feet as they play hide and seek,
Echoing back her heart in its joy;
　And see her hands as they give a toy.

None but a mother can see or hear,
　For every movement and look is dear;
To you it sounds like birds in the air,
　While I hear " Mamma " everywhere.

HOME LIGHTS.

THAT light in your home is a welcome,
   And it shines in the dark bright and clear,
To tell you that hearts are waiting
   For one who is always dear.

You feel so sure of the signal,
   You scarce think of it any more,
But the night it burns out you 'll miss it,
   As the sailor his light on the shore.

The hand may be white and dimpled,
  Or old and brown and thin,
That lights your lamp by the window,
  But there 's the same welcome within.

So be careful just how you enter,
  With bright cheery greeting and smile,
'T is home-light—if only a candle,
  And home love you will have but a while.

THE BOY'S GREETING.

MOTHER, I send my love to thee
 Over the wires of steel ;
I feel the pressure of thy hand,
 Its warmth to me is real.

Though high and many the hills between,
 The old home still is dear,
This little home will soon be mine
 To hold and have you near.

Be brave, be calm, for thy boy's sake,
 He 's true as steel to thee,
And never forgets the lessons learned,
 Nor the prayer he said at thy knee.

BROWN AND HAZEL.

BROWN—brown hair and hazel eyes
　　Bonny, beaming, bright;
　　Skipping off away she hies,
　　Now quite out of sight.

Darling, dancing, daring eyes,
　　Flashing in the light;
Weary, wistful, winsome eyes,
　　Go to sleep—'t is night.

They have lights that come and go,
   Twinkling, starry eyes,
Filled with tears they touch me so,
   Filling me with sighs.

Bright or wistful, sad or gay,
   Such the forms they wear,
Changing even in their play,
   Hazel eyes—brown hair.

ADORNED.

LOOSEN the pearls from her fair young throat,
　　The buds from her gold-brown hair;
Neither necklace nor bud in beauty can vie
　　With His gift, my jewel rare.

Nothing becomes thee, child, to wear,
　　While thy voice hath youth in its note,
Like the braids formed of thine own sunny hair,
　　With the ringlets encircling thy throat.

With the blossom tinted by God's own hand,
　　Does the blush on thy cheek agree;
As thou standest in sweet simplicity clad,
　　Thou 'rt adorned, my child, to me.

44

A DREAM.

I THOUGHT I heard the deep-voiced sea
  Chide me in my dream ;
And for something I had left undone
  The moon held back her beam.

But on my ear fell mystic tones,
  As from some holy choir ;
Their voices sounding far and near,
  Did my very soul inspire.

45

Like the life-laden seed of an autumn flower,
  Its wings spread on the wind,
I was borne aloft in my car of thought,
  'Till I had left the world behind.

In the gentle breeze that sped me on,
  The broken clouds would mend;
And as I sailed from land to land,
  Old scenes with new did blend.

The mountain peaks were far below,
  And rivers, like a thread,
Linked sea and land and distant shore—
  A mystic scene far-spread.

The pale moon, very full and white,
  Was soaring now in air ;
And the misty rain on the mountain slope,
  Froze in feathery plumage fair.

By day a bow in the cloud was set,
  At night no sound was heard,
Save echoing faint in the clear still air
  Came back the note of a bird.

And when I wandered back to earth,
  And reached my home again,
The peace I found in my fancy's flight,
  Helped me forget grief's pain.

The same tone from the holy choir
    Fell on my listening ear;
And though in my dream I was high and far,
    I had not thought of fear.

And as I pass through life's real maze,
    In sunlight or in shade,
May peace and hope shine always bright,
    And I be not afraid.

EASTER.

ITH your memories full of mourning,
  Will you always bring me pain,
Can you ever, joyous Easter,
  Be the same to me again?

Will I always for their voices
  Be listening in my song,
And feel their touch while waiting
  Through the days and nights so long?

If I could hear them singing
  While I am weeping here,
I might then stop my sighing,
  And brush away the tear.

49

We 'll meet again—who whispers,
  That I may catch the tone,
And feel hope's first assurance
  While waiting here alone?

This thought is so consoling,
  The promise is so sweet,
With faith I 'll hedge it round about,—
  I 'll know them when we meet.

Without hope, then, shall I sorrow?
  Nay, we shall know again ;
With the Lord in blest reunion,
  In his presence, without pain.

EASTER.

WHEN cometh Easter morning,
    Give of thy best gifts,
Gladdening in some home a heart
    Where the burden never lifts.

Speak only words of kindness;
    Lend only happy smiles;
Give consolation where there 's woe,
    The look that care beguiles.

Give all then thou art able
    Of word or look or gold;
The Master's smile, His word, " well done,"
    Will pay thee many fold.

SPRING.

WHEN the snows are gone and the winter past,
  And the days are growing longer,
What shall I do with the lengthened time
  Until my heart gets stronger?

How shall I welcome the glad spring-time,
  Its mild and mellow mist,
Its tints, its tone, its tenderness,
  And to its laughter list?

SPRING.

How shall I sing the songs again
    That tuned to her childish voice?
Where shall I go to bury pain
    And in God's ways rejoice?

By forgetting self I will go on,
    Helping where'er I can,
Sharing the stroke on others sent,
    Because it is Thy plan.

SPRING.

And thus in peace I 'll welcome spring—
   All seasons first and last.
They but do His work, fulfil His will.
   Bring they blossom or blast.

WELCOME.

COME when the day is over,
   Or when 't is just begun :
Come at the break of morning,
  Or at the set of sun.

Come when we are weary,
  Or when with strength imbued :
Come when sick and saddened,
  Or by health renewed.

Welcome in joy or sorrow,
　　In the shadow or the light ;
Whether we 're twining cypress,
　　Or the holly-wreath to-night.

In the welcome that we give thee,
　　There is set no day or hour ;
And thy coming would have no ending,
　　Were it wholly in our power.

And when life lasts no longer
　　Let Mizpah be our prayer,
For sisters' love which changeth not
　　Is blessed, sweet, and rare.

NATURE.

THE sunbeam warmed the daisies,
And hid in the blades of grass;
While the violets blew in the meadows green,
Where the gentle zephyrs pass.

The stream played o'er the pebbles,
The polished rocks between;
And the rusty cup, by the clear cold spring,
Hung low in its mossy green.

57

The sweet briar blushed on the mountain,
   To its delicate, shell-pink tint ;
And the diamonds paled and sparkled,
   As the sun shone on the flint.

In their sweet small way, the wild flowers,
   And the songsters in the air,
Singing out in full from their tiny throats—
   All laughed at blank despair.

NEWS.

OH the notes so white and dainty,
    That the wind to-day did blow,
In the broad sweep over the housetop,
    Coming in flakes of snow.

59

Bringing gentle reminders
   Of the year so ready to go,
Tender memories of changing time,
   In its busy ebb and flow.

Telling of August harvest,
   Of young April's sudden showers,
Of June, the month of roses,
   And May's bouquet of flowers.

Of December's holly berries,
   And October's yellow leaf,
Of days when skies were cloudless,
   And the wheat was in the sheaf.

Bring me more news to-morrow,
　You dancing, fairy flakes ;
I 've friends I am anxious to hear from,
　From the Gulf 'way up to the lakes.

AWHILE.

BLIND with tears,
　　Sick with fears,
We sit all alone with our sorrow.
　　This fair face,
　　This lovely grace,
To be hidden from earth to-morrow.

　　Fallen asleep
　　Ere learning to weep,
Or in grief's pain to share ;
　　In beauty immortal,
　　Within heaven's portal,
Just gone before us there.

　　Leaving her play,
　　In His arms she lay,
He hushed her gently to sleep ;
　　Sweetly at rest,
　　At home with the blest,
'T is only awhile that we weep.

TALITHA CUMI.

IN Jairus' joy there was a pang,
   There was hope e'en in my despair,
Though mine was taken and his child left,—
      Both young, both fair.

My hour is past, my anguish o'er,
   While his was but deferred,
And all the time my heart was crushed,
      " Doubt not," I heard.

" Come, child,"—He gently spoke to one,
   And called to earth again.
To mine, too, " Come,"—but that meant heaven,
      Past grief, past pain.

64

Once more " Talitha " He will call,
  Her sleeping form will raise,
In glorious guise, but still unchanged,
    To Him all praise.

NOW.

PRAISE me while I can hear you,
  Bring kiss and smile while I live;
Your treasures of care and affection,
  Now only you truly can give.

Clasp my hand while it thrills me,
  Its strength or its tremor feel,
With the hand I give, my heart is,
  It chills in the grasp of steel.

Bring flowers while I can see them;
  Let their fragrance speak of your love;
Why wait till, still and silent,
  My spirit nothing can move?

Neglected, our hearts faint and famish,
   For love is their wine and bread ;
Starve not nor chill with your coldness,
   Too late for your kindness,—when dead.

ABSENCE.

HAS ever the scent of a simple flower,
　　Though very faint its perfume,
Made you feel sick and all alone,
　　Just you—and the world in gloom ?

Have you ever felt in the summer's breath,
　　Though only a zephyr passed,
Faint and trembling and cold with fear,
　　As though the breath were a blast.

Have you ever gazed on a passing shower,
  And felt you could drop a tear,
As the music sweet of its plashing drops
  Brought back to you memories dear?

Have you ever felt lonely, with gloom oppressed,
  Amid the happy and strong?
Of all your life the loneliest there
  When thrown with the joyous throng?

'T is this that hearts feel in absence drear
  Of loved ones in heaven or earth;
'T is sigh after sigh—and heart crying out,
  The same all along from our birth.

THOUGHTS.

IF it be true that thoughts have wings,
  Then think them as we will,
To ourselves—or spoken aloud,
  Some other heart they 'll fill.

Either for good or harm they 've gone
  Straight to another's breast,
They 've left our lips and have flown away,
  Like a bird flying home to its nest.

Sooner or later our lives they review,
    Those we smile on and flatter,
And when we 've forgotten, remember anew
    And uncover the seed we scatter.

And so we 've no secrets after all,
    It would not be well if we could,
As all are the children of one family here,
    'T was not intended we should.

TIRED.

THERE comes a wish in every life,
  Be it gay or grave ;
There comes a longing after rest,
  Be we weak or brave.

Only tired—even of self,
  Weary of friend and foe,
And nothing we do brings us the rest
  That it did some time ago.

And it is right that this is so,
  The planning is all His own ;
It helps us to give up this life
  For the life-seat round His throne.

WHILE YOU MAY.

THE old-fashioned lilacs,
>   So they say,
>   Filled the air with perfume
>   Every day.
>   When the lilacs come again
Draw the curtain, lift the pane,
Breathe in their fragrance while they stay.

>   Young rose leaves are tender,
>   So they say—
>   Leaves oft expanding
>   In a day.
Then await the coming shower,
With budding in its power,
Have the beauteous roses while you may.

73

In the heat of summer sun,
  So they say,
Some stem all the others will outrun
  In a day.
And the stem that runs the first
Will bear a bud to burst,
And add another rose to our bouquet.

The echo 's on the hill,
  So they say,
Yet heard down by the mill
  Every day.
As the echo comes 't will go,
Just how we do not know,
And so it is with all we do or say.

QUAINT.

S O very few faults and so very quaint
Is my little old-fashioned girl;
So neat and sweet whenever we meet,
Though she wears neither
bang nor curl.

Her dolls all have their own
right place,
Their dresses are spotless
as snow,
And just which sash belongs
to each,
This old-fashioned girl
will know.

75

She 's neither large, nor yet is she small,
    This quaint little six years old;
Toys all put away after play each day,
    Although she has never been told.

GROWING OLD.

NOT so lightly trips my footstep
 As it did in days of yore,
And there may be threads of silver
 'Mid the tresses brown before.

Yet how much they are mistaken
 Who mistake this change for me,
For 't is but the house I live in ;
 Houses crumble as you see.

77

It may be that lines are breaking
   On the brow so smooth before;
Houses sure will crack and tumble,
   When of care there is full store.

If the heart be young and hopeful,
   What if then the house be old?
Youthful heart, whose fire is glowing,
   Ne'er will let the house grow cold.

FANCY.

L OOSEN fancy, let her roam
  Till somewhere she find a home;
Help her break her leaden string
And soar high upon the wing.

Let her dance upon the spray,
Learn to sing in accents gay;
Learn to warble, learn to trill,
Till our very soul she thrill.

Of despair is fancy born,
Comes from tears as rose from thorn ;
Loose her, lift her on the wing,
Help her, if you can, to sing.

Lift poor fancy from the dust,
Teach her if you can to trust ;
In her rhythm let her go,
And in song forget her woe.

A GREENWOOD TALE.

UNDER the hawthorn where the sun is pale,
    The fairies told a marvellous tale

Of the eglantine—of the early rose,
And where the four-leaved clover grows ;

Of leafy trees, where hidden between
Could always vernal bloom be seen ;

Of weeping willows nodding their plumes,
When in the village are brides and grooms.

They told of the robin's rendezvous,
Each to the other always true ;

Of the humming-bird in his plumage gay,
Wishing his winters were always May,

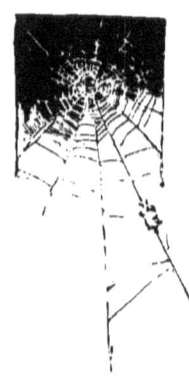

And the butterfly in his purple and gold,
When his gauzy wings in the light unfold ;

And the busy spiders, black and gray,
Who weave their webs all in a day ;

Of tiny pebbles washed by the stream,
Till round and smooth and white they gleam.

What wonderful things a fairy sees,
Out in the greenwood under the trees.

OUR BOYS.

IN size they are such grown-up men,
  In voice, in look, in ways,
  Yet we 'd turn the long years back again
    again
  To their noisy boyish plays.

His sweet " Ah Goo " can you ever forget,
  Or when he first found he 'd hands;
And then how you flew, all in earnest too,
  To obey his slightest commands.

Can't you see the rows of his little toes,
  With their pink and pearly nails;
And looking down to leather from kid,
  Almost think that your eyesight fails.

What would you give for a footprint now,
 And a stocking splashed to the knee;
Instead of the boots with their pointed toes
 And the flat seams you 're forced to see?

Or the deep round linen that left us room,
 To kiss him under his chin;
While tying his bow with ends in a row,
 And tucking the loops within.

But come what will of inches still,
 They can't take from us the past;
And we 'll walk by his side, our boy, our pride,
 For they all must be men at last.

TWILIGHT.

THE day is passing over me,
  And twilight, like a gauze,
Shuts out yon field and lane and tree,
  And life seems at a pause.

Shadows fall about my feet,
  Yet neither day nor night;
The birds have ceased their warbling sweet,
  Yet neither dark nor light.

The only interval of rest,
From care and duty free;
Of all the hours I love it best,
My heart returns to thee.

Twilight, the hour of quiet peace,
The only hour for me;
When other claims their clamors cease,
And I 'm alone with thee.

FORWARD.

Look forward instead of backward,
  To the future instead of the past ;
'T is all that will send you onward
  To find rest and peace at last.

To go backward you 'll only stumble
  Over the past of regret,
And the " ifs " and " buts " cannot help you,
  Though past sadness you cannot forget.

The present looks on to the future,
  And to each and all that we do,
From now until life 's ended
  We will have to bid adieu.

MY SONG.

There 's a song in my heart both sweet and sad,
  Though its words are never said ;
Voice out of breath, and life out of tune,
  Those who sang with me are dead.

Thoughts of the past on tremulous lips,
  In low notes wooing despair ;
Vibrant with feeling never expressed,
  Plaintively filling the air.

Its tenderest tones soft language lends,
  To voices we hear in our dreams ;
Together again with inspiring theme,
  Our voices are mingled, it seems.

BEAUTY.

Nature to some hearts so much supplies,
The inward goodness outward lack defies ;
True beauty doth some spirits so refine,
That what we yearn for—their's a gift divine.

TAUGHT BY THE FLOWERS.

HE wild flowers blush in their beauty,
    Out of sight and touch of man ;
        Fulfilling each day their duty,
            Their part in God's wonderful
            plan.

The busiest honey bee feeding,
    Sheltering the beauteous bird,
Welcoming shower and sunshine—
    By gentle zephyrs stirred.

Then nothing of God's need be idle;
There 's work enough for all—
If the flower has part in God's service,
To us is the same loving call.

SHADOWS.

SHADOWS lie about our feet,
   And darken all delight;
In midnight's gloom despair we meet
   And hope seems lost to sight.

Sunniest hearts have wintry days,
   When sadness leaves its pain;
Yet God helps in so many ways
   That hope comes back again.

Spring and winter bring their gleam
   Of sunlight and of snow;
Hearts' unrest will seem a dream
   And faith make hope to glow.

93

THE MIRROR.

A H glass, with your wondrous power to trace
    All that you found so fair,
Why did you not hold her sweet young face
  While she was looking there?

In evening's soft light or morning's beam
　　You caught each change in her face,
The shades and the gloss of her sunny hair,
　　And her movements of childish grace.

The drooping lids with their lashes long,
　　Her eyes of violet blue,
Her sweet fresh mouth just ripe for song,
　　And cheeks of delicate hue.

If you knew how empty you look and how cold,
　　With your ribbons decked out so fair—
A glass, but a glass, so hard and so cold,
　　You would not be standing there.

Yet still I am standing, still waiting here
  For a face that is young and so fair,
But gaze as I will, the only face near
  Is my own, all pale with despair.

CAN IT BE?

THEY tell me of anguish mellowed
  To thoughtful sadness sweet,
They tell of tears when trembling
  Oft lightened by smiles we meet.

They tell me of sorrow vanished,
  Grief healed with time and age,
And nothing but scars remaining
  On memory's deep, wide page.

They tell me of spirit troubled,
  Finding its sorrow has flown,
And how the sigh is forgotten
  To which the sad heart was prone.

GOOD-NIGHT AND GOOD-BYE.

GOOD-NIGHT and good-bye, you dear old year,
   I did so think to go with you
That I told you all the secrets I had,
   Never asking that you would be true.

You seemed so young compared with me,
   That to watch without you to-night—
Why you should go first, and I wait here—
   Seems so unreal—Is it right?

We kept so close through the chilly days,
　　And all through the summer sun;
I always had so much to tell,
　　And you 're gone ere my story 's begun.

You 've been so patient, you dear old year;
　　How you tried to make me glad!
You brought me new friends who had sorrowed, too,
　　Now happy, who once were sad.

I owe you so much, and now you 're gone,
　　Is there nothing that I can do?
Can I not help some stricken one
　　Who 'd be glad to have gone with you?

Then trust me, old year, I will do my best
  In act, in word, and thought ;
And as God measures both your span and mine,
  I 'll trust Him till home I 'm brought.

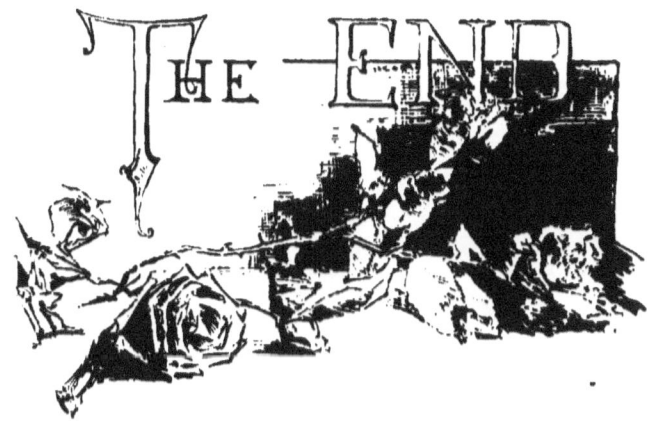

www.ingramcontent.com/pod-product-compliance
Lightning Source LLC
Chambersburg PA
CBHW032202010726
47493CB00008BA/2795